BE
STILL
AND KNOW THAT
I AM GOD.

PSALM 46:10

BILL DONAHUE,
AMY AND JUDGE REINHOLD

WILLOW
Willow Creek Resources

BE
STILL

Requests for information should be addressed to:
Willow Creek Association
P.O. Box 3188, Barrington, Illinois 60011-3188

ISBN 0-744-19248-X

All Scripture quotations, unless otherwise indicated, are taken from the *Holy Bible, Today's New International Version*®. *TNIV*®. Copyright © 2002, 2004 by International Bible Society. Used by permission of Zondervan. All rights reserved.

Scripture quotations marked (KJV) are taken from the *Holy Bible, King James Version*. In the Public Domain.

Scripture quotations marked (MSG) are taken from THE MESSAGE. Copyright © by Eugene H. Peterson 1993, 1994, 1995, 1996, 2000, 2001, 2002. Used by permission of NavPress Publishing Group.

Scripture quotations marked (NKJV) are taken from the *Holy Bible, New King James Version*. Copyright © 1982 by Thomas Nelson, Inc. Used by permission. All rights reserved.

Scripture quotations marked (NLT) are taken from the *Holy Bible, New Living Translation,* copyright © 1996, 2004. Used by permission of Tyndale House Publishers, Inc., Wheaton, IL 60189 USA. All rights reserved.

Illustrations by Lezle Williams, www.laughingcrowstudio.com

Cover and interior design by 32 design, www.32design.com

07 08 09 10 11 12 13 • 10 9 8 7 6 5 4 3 2 1

Printed in the United States of America

contents

How to Use This Discussion Guide   5

Introduction
Fall More Deeply in Love with God   7

Session One
What Is Contemplative Prayer?   13

Session Two
Silence and Scripture: The Core of Contemplative Prayer   31

Session Three
Lectio Divina: The Practice of Contemplative Prayer   41

Session Four
Connecting Personally with God   53

Next Steps   65

Additional Resources   69

About the Authors   71

HOW TO USE THIS DISCUSSION GUIDE

GROUP SIZE

Be Still is designed to be experienced in a group setting, such as Sunday school classes or small group gatherings. To ensure that everyone has enough time to participate in discussions, we recommend that groups be no larger than six to twelve people.

Each person should have his or her own participant's guide, which includes prompts for DVD segments, directions for activities, discussion questions and a list of resources for further exploration.

FORMAT OPTIONS

Be Still includes four one-hour sessions. You may experience each one separately in consecutive meetings, or they can be completed in combination: for example, two two-hour meetings, or one four-hour meeting. If you combine sessions, be sure to allow additional time for breaks.

Timing

The time notations—for example, (12 minutes)—indicate the actual playing time of DVD segments and the suggested times for each activity or discussion. Adhering to the suggested times will enable you to complete each session in sixty minutes. If you have additional time, you may wish to allow more time for discussion and activities.

Facilitation

One of the best parts about *Be Still* is that no one has to be an expert in order to lead a group. However, your group should choose one person to be responsible for stopping and starting the DVD at the appropriate times, and for keeping track of time during discussions and activities. This person may also read questions aloud and facilitate discussions, making sure everyone has a chance to participate.

intRODUCtiON

Fall More Deeply in Love with God

S top for a minute. Take a deep breath. Do you hear that? That's quiet. That's you taking back one small moment of quiet from your noisy day.

Everyone wants more peace. And we need to learn to fight the weapons of mass *distraction* in order to attain that peace. Have you ever had one of those "aha" moments in which you realize something has got to change? A friend relayed one of those moments recently. She was running around the kitchen with her cell phone in hand, trying to heat leftovers in the microwave to eat in the car on the way to a meeting she was already late for. Her home phone rang, and the answering machine started blaring, just as she was dialing her cell phone to tell the people she was meeting she was running late. The only problem was that instead of dialing the number on the phone in her hand, she had punched it into the microwave keypad!

Do you ever feel like no matter what you do, you just never catch up? In the fast-paced life we live, it's easy for all of us to get trapped in the tyranny of the urgent.

Before we started our *Be Still* journey, our prayer lives consisted of hurried requests lobbed to God as we dashed out the door, stop-and-go prayers during rush-hour traffic and running down a list of needs for family and friends just before bed.

We heard the same frustrations from people around us. They needed more peace in their lives, were disappointed with themselves for not spending enough time in the Bible and desired a deeper intimacy with God.

To us, a much-needed antidote to our fast-paced lives was the practice of contemplative prayer. We first experienced the peace and power of contemplative prayer in our small group Bible study. One of the leaders introduced us to a form of contemplative prayer called *lectio divina* [lek-tsea-oh di-veen-ah]. *Lectio divina* is Latin for "divine" or "sacred" reading and has actually been a part of church life for centuries! Many people in the early church were illiterate or did not have Bibles, so *lectio divina* offered a way of listening to Scripture that would stay in the mind and resonate in the heart throughout the day.

Lectio divina is a structure of prayer that uses Scripture and silence to invite God's presence and direction into our lives. In *lectio divina* we discover that there is no place in our hearts—no interior corner or closet—that cannot be opened and offered to God.

Lectio divina is much like tuning the radio to your favorite station and singing the song you hear the rest of the day. By really listening to the Scripture as it is read slowly and deliberately, and letting it soak in during a time of silence, you learn to tune your heart to the "gentle whisper" of God (1 Kings 19:12).

> *Lectio divina is a structure of prayer that uses Scripture and silence to invite God's presence and direction into our lives.*

We know it is vital to study the Bible for solid context and doctrinal truth, but it is just as important to learn how to meditate on the Word and allow it to permeate our lives and the decisions we make. When we listen with our hearts in this way, we can't help but draw closer to the heart of Christ and be transformed and renewed by the Living Word of God.

If we really want to know God, we will seek Him. As we start to enjoy His divine companionship, experience His peace and trust His direction, we will crave more of Him in every area of our lives. Eventually we will come to a place where He will ask us what we want and we will simply say, "You, Lord—not your blessings, not what you can do for us—only You."

Be Still provides a retreat from our busyness and distractions so we can deepen our understanding of the Word of God in our lives. You don't have to be a super scholar or saint to experience this type of prayer and intimacy with God. Contemplative prayer is simple. You just have to look for times to stop and grab *Be Still* moments instead of your cell phone. You have these moments throughout your day, but if you don't make time to recognize them, you will miss God's little gifts of grace and peace.

Taste and see that the LORD is good.

Psalm 34:8a

You might protest you don't have time for contemplative prayer or worry that it is a frivolous escape from the world. However, contemplative prayer is an essential way to improve the quality of any busy person's life, giving you permission to resign as CEO of your life, allowing God to have a say in everything you do and equipping you to better serve those around you.

We are not experts, but simply fellow travelers who have a hunch that in this information age, our lives are probably not going to slow down and become less complicated unless we make some deliberate choices. Our ultimate goal is to help each other learn to rest in the Lord even amidst the busyness of life.

—*Amy and Judge Reinhold*

SESSION ONE

What Is Contemplative Prayer?

introduction

This session explores the concept of contemplative prayer and how this kind of prayer uses Scripture and silence to help us connect with God. Contemplative prayer invites us to slow down and step back from the distractions of a hectic and stressful world that screams at us all day long, drowning out the still, small voice of God. We are invited to learn more about what it means to "be still, and know that I am God" (Psalm 46:10).

DISCUSSION (10 minutes)

What is your first memory of prayer? Share a serious or funny story about an experience in prayer.

PLAY DVD (10 minutes)

Insert the DVD and select "Contemplative Prayer" on the main menu.

Press PAUSE when the title screen "What Is Contemplative Prayer?" appears.

Notes

We must concentrate on

knowing God: the more we

know Him the more we want to

know Him. And as knowledge

is commonly the measure of

love, the deeper and wider our

knowledge, the greater will be our

love. And if our love of God is

great, we shall love Him equally

in our joy or sorrow.

Brother Lawrence

DISCUSSION (5 minutes)

What is your reaction to the idea of slowing down to listen for God's "divine whisper" through Scripture?

PLAY DVD (6 minutes)

Press PLAY to resume watching the segment at the title screen, "What Is Contemplative Prayer?"

Press PAUSE when the title screen "Historical Overview" appears.

Notes

DISCUSSION (10 minutes)

The DVD includes several descriptions of contemplative prayer, a sampling of which is listed below. Which description strikes a chord in you?

- ❖ Listening to God's call through Scripture
- ❖ Attentiveness to God's divine whisper
- ❖ Sitting in stillness
- ❖ Listening in humility
- ❖ Being fulfilled by God
- ❖ Leaning into a passage letting the Lord teach me
- ❖ To know, "I AM THAT I AM" (Exodus 3:14 KJV)

These descriptions reveal a need to slow down and listen to God. What would it take for you to begin to slow down and be quiet with God?

Thou hast formed

us for thyself, and our hearts

are restless till they find

rest in thee.

St. Augustine

INDIVIDUAL REFLECTION (5 minutes)

Reflecting on the discussion you just had, take a few moments to write your thoughts about how busy and noisy your own life is. Use the space below to:

❖ Imagine what contemplative prayer would bring to your life.

❖ List one hope or expectation you have as you consider implementing this kind of prayer in your life.

❖ Identify the biggest obstacle that stands in your way.

REFLECTION

For me, contemplative prayer would bring. . .

My expectation and hope is that . . .

The biggest obstacle that might keep me from experiencing this kind of prayer is . . .

DISCVSSIOΠ (10 minvtEs)

Take a few moments to briefly share what you wrote down during the Individual Reflection experience.

OPTIONAL DVD SEGMENT AND DISCUSSION

If you have more than 60 minutes for your discussion, take about 15 minutes to watch and discuss this segment on the history of contemplative prayer.

PLAY DVD (10 minutes)

Press PLAY to resume watching the segment at the title screen, "Historical Overview."

Press STOP when the title screen, "The Need for Contemplative Prayer" appears. (This is where you will begin the DVD in the Session Two.)

DISCUSSION (5 minutes)

What stood out to you as you heard stories about Christians throughout history who practiced contemplative prayer?

Notes

We must in all our prayers
carefully avoid wishing to confine God
to certain circumstances, or prescribe
to God the time, place or mode of
action . . . For before we offer up any
petition for ourselves, we ask that
God's will may be done, and by
so doing place our will in
subordination to God's.

John Calvin

GROUP PRACTICE (5 minutes)

Close the discussion by spending two to five minutes together in silence. Choose one person to be the timekeeper. Begin by reading a short psalm or other portion of Scripture aloud and praying for the Holy Spirit to lead you. After a few minutes, the timekeeper closes the meeting by simply saying, "Thank you for this time together, Lord. In Jesus' name, amen." (Note: If this is your first experience of silence together, the two to five minutes might seem much longer. That's okay! If you have more than sixty minutes for your meeting, you may want to take a few minutes to talk about the experience and discuss how the time of silence made you feel.)

INDIVIDUAL PRACTICE

Between now and the next session, set aside at least one time to be quietly alone with God.

Find a quiet place. This could be a room at home or someplace away from home, as long as it is quiet and free of distractions.

Begin with five to ten minutes of silence. Before you start a time of silence, it might be helpful to set a timer so you are not distracted by having to look at your watch. As you begin, take a few slow, deep breaths. When you inhale, think of the Holy Spirit breathing life and peace into your body. As you exhale, remember the verse that says to cast all your anxiety on Him (1 Peter 5:7). Be aware of God's presence and ask for His help to remove any distractions and help you focus on Him. If you find your to-do list continues to be the only thing you can think of, take a few minutes to write it down and then let it go. (It will still be there after you spend quality time with God!)

> *Cast all your anxiety on him because he cares for you.*
>
> *1 Peter 5:7 (TNIV)*

Be still and listen. There are times when music, reading, prayer requests and journaling are important, but don't fill the silence with anything just now. Try not to control the experience or place expectations on God (how you want Him to speak to you, what you want Him to say, how powerful it must be, etc.). To the degree that you are able, simply relax and enjoy God's presence.

Reflect on your experience. Allow five to ten minutes for this. After your time of silence, reflect on any thoughts or feelings you had. Maybe you felt anxious or had a hard time staying focused. Maybe you sensed God's comfort or encouragement. Perhaps a specific person or situation you've been avoiding came to mind. It could also be that nothing happened—you simply were still and enjoyed God's presence.

You may want to write a few notes about your experience. For example, "It was harder than I thought to be still and quiet," "I feel drawn to silence but it scares me too" or "I felt very peaceful and want to keep that feeling throughout my day."

End your time. Close your time and transition gently back into your day. You may want to offer a simple prayer of thanks to God for this gift of time with Him. Or you might take a walk, listen to music or simply have a cup of coffee. Avoid making an abrupt shift from stillness and silence into a flurry of activity. Allow yourself to ease into anything you do next, being mindful of the time you just spent with God.

You might also want to consider setting aside another time to be alone with God. Mark your calendar before other people, tasks and events have a chance to fill up all your time.

When a man is born from above, the
life of the Son of God is born in him,
and he can either starve that life or
nourish it. Prayer is the way the life of
God is nourished. Our ordinary views
of prayer are not found in the New
Testament. We look upon prayer as a
means of getting things for ourselves;
the Bible's idea of prayer is that we
may get to know God Himself.

Oswald Chambers

Session Two

Silence and Scripture: The Core of Contemplative Prayer

introduction

In this session you will look at the need for contemplative prayer, especially when life is filled with noise and cluttered with busyness. You will face your fear of silence and learn to hear the voice of God in Scripture.

Discussion (10 minutes)

If you could remove one major stress from your life right now, what would that be?

PLAY DVD (8 minutes)

Insert the DVD and select "Contemplative Prayer" on the main menu. Fast-forward through the first twelve minutes (previously viewed in Session One). A title screen will appear that reads "The Need for Contemplative Prayer." Press PLAY.

Press PAUSE when the title screen "Fear of Silence" appears.

DISCUSSION (10 minutes)

Take a few moments to discuss the following questions:

- ❖ What is your initial reaction to what the speakers said about silence?

- ❖ Do you believe such stillness and silence are really possible in your life? In your group?

- ❖ What might be different about your life (or your group) if you practiced slowing down and getting quiet enough to hear God's "still, small voice"?

Notes

Oh, the joys of those who do not
follow the advice of the wicked, or
stand around with sinners, or join in
with mockers. But they delight in the
law of the LORD, meditating on it day
and night. They are like trees planted
along the riverbank, bearing fruit each
season. Their leaves never wither, and
they prosper in all they do.

Psalm 1:1-3 (NLT)

PLAY DVD (12 minutes)

Press PLAY to resume watching the segment at the title screen "Fear of Silence." Listen carefully as the speakers describe the following:

* ❖ Silence

* ❖ The differences between Christian and non-Christian meditation

* ❖ How God speaks to us through Scripture

You might want to jot down a few notes about each of these areas to prepare for the discussion that follows.

Press PAUSE when the title screen "The Fruit of Contemplative Prayer" appears. You are finished with the DVD for this session.

Notes

DISCUSSION (7 minutes)

Learning to read the Bible for *inspiration* is just as important as reading for *information* and will change the way you relate to God and hear His voice. Richard Foster described God's voice as always being consistent with the tone, spirit and content of God's voice in the Bible.

❖ Is it new for you to experience God's Word this way?

❖ What thoughts come to mind as you consider listening to God by meditating on Scripture?

*If we really want to pray, we must
first learn to listen: for in the silence
of the heart God speaks. And to be
able to see that silence, to be able
to hear God, we need a clean heart.
Let us listen to God, to what He has
to say. We cannot speak unless we
have listened, unless we have made
our connection with God. From the
fullness of the heart, the mouth will
speak, the mind will think.*

Mother Teresa

Praying the Scripture is not judged by how much you read but the way you read. If you read quickly, it will benefit you little. You will be like a bee that merely skims the surface of a flower. Instead, in this new way of reading with prayer, you will become as the bee that penetrates into the depths of the flower. You plunge deeply within to remove its deepest nectar.

Madame Guyon

GROUP PRACTICE (10 minutes)

Ask someone to slowly read Psalm 16:11 aloud four times, taking a minute of silence between each reading to really let the words permeate your thoughts. Don't try to interpret or apply the words; just listen.

DISCUSSION (3 minutes)

Briefly recap the group practice:

- ❖ What did you experience?

- ❖ Were you peaceful, distracted or uncomfortable?

CLOSE IN PRAYER (5 minutes)

Close in prayer. If there are other group issues that need to be addressed, we encourage you to address them after closing in prayer.

Lectio Divina:

The Practice of Contemplative Prayer

INTRODUCTION

Now that you have a greater understanding of contemplative prayer and have practiced being still and quiet, it's time to dig deeper.

In this session you'll learn the ancient, biblical yet fresh practice of *lectio divina* or "divine reading." Christians throughout history have used this practice to draw near to God and to one another in community.

As you move into this session, it may be helpful to remember the instructions the Lord gave Joshua:

> *Keep this Book of the Law always on your lips; meditate on it day and night, so that you may be careful to do everything written in it. Then you will be prosperous and successful* (Joshua 1:8).

Since Christian meditation is about filling the mind and not about "emptying" the mind, the best thing with which to fill the mind is God's truth. The Bible is central to the practice of Christian meditation and prayer. Learn to hear God and meet Him in His Word.

DISCUSSION (5 minutes)

What role, if any, did the Bible play in your life growing up? Did you read it as a family, by yourself, or just hear it read at church services, weddings or funerals?

The Bible is not an end in itself,

but a means to bring men to an

intimate and satisfying knowledge of

God, that they may enter into Him,

that they may delight in His

Presence, may taste and know the

inner sweetness of the very God

Himself in the core and center

of their hearts.

A.W. Tozer

Oh, how I love your law!

I meditate on it all day long.

Psalm 119:97

PLAY DVD (17 minutes)

Insert the DVD and select "Contemplative Prayer" on the main menu. Fast-forward through the first thirty-seven minutes or so (37:30 on the DVD timer). The title screen "Family" will appear, and Mark Brewer will begin speaking.

After the song is complete, stop the DVD when the verse from Habakkuk 2:20 appears on the screen.

NOTES

DISCUSSION (8 minutes)

In which of the following three areas do you see the greatest opportunity for impact from practicing contemplative prayer?

1. In my family—I believe our family would benefit greatly because . . .

2. In the church—I believe my church (or the church worldwide) would benefit greatly because . . .

3. In the world—I believe that contemplative prayer would allow me to impact the world because . . .

PLAY DVD (8 minutes)

Return to the main menu and select "Small Groups." In this segment you will learn more about the process of *lectio divina*.

STOP the DVD when the title screen with Jeremiah 6:16 appears.

Notes

GROUP PRACTICE (15 minutes)

Use the following process to experience *lectio divina* together.

Select a passage. You may select a passage from the list below, or choose your own. You may want to use a verse or passage from a study you are doing in your group, or you might focus more deeply on a verse you heard recently in a message at your church. Whatever you choose, the passage should be no longer than four to ten sentences.

Suggested passages:

- ❖ Psalm 119:105–8
- ❖ Proverbs 16:1–3
- ❖ Matthew 7:7–12
- ❖ Romans 12:9–13

Read the passage aloud four times. Have one person read the passage aloud—*slowly and deliberately*. Between each reading, allow a time of silence to let the words permeate your heart. Follow the steps below throughout the readings.

- ❖ ***Read***: On the first reading, simply listen to the words read aloud.
- ❖ ***Reflect***: On the second reading, ask, *What in the passage touches my life today?*
- ❖ ***Respond***: After the third reading, ask yourself, *What is God inviting me to do today?*

- ❖ **Rest**: During the fourth and final reading, ask nothing; simply rest in the presence of the Lord and experience His guidance through the Word.

- ❖ **Share***: Share what God has spoken to you through His Word.

- ❖ **Pray**: Pray for each person to walk in the power of the living Word revealed. The session ends when the last person has prayed.

* There is no obligation to share with your group, but if you are comfortable doing so, share what God has spoken to you. This deepens the experience for everyone in the group.

If you have more than sixty minutes, take a few minutes to talk about your experience together or to write down what God spoke into your heart through His Word. Some groups might choose to begin a group journal, noting what God speaks into their lives through specific passages the group experiences through *lectio divina*. It can be exciting to look back in later meetings to see how God's Word continues to be active in each other's lives.

> *But the LORD is in his holy temple: let all the earth keep silence before him.*
>
> *Habakkuk 2:20 (KJV)*

CLOSE IN PRAYER (2 minutes)

Were I a preacher, I should,
above all other things, preach the
practice of the presence of God.

Brother Lawrence

Connecting
Personally with God

iΠτRodVctioΠ

Lectio divina is not just for small groups; it can also be practiced alone. In this session you will discover how this practice can deepen your personal prayer life and how it will help you hear the voice of God for guidance, correction, comfort and peace.

DiscVssioΠ (5 minVtes)

Think back on your spiritual journey. Regardless of where you are at this point, there were probably people who influenced you in some way to pursue God. Perhaps it was a friend or relative or even an author whose writings pierced your soul or softened your heart.

Break up into groups of two or three. Describe the person or persons who have played a significant role in your faith journey.

PLAY DVD (10 minVtes)

Insert the DVD and select "Cloud of Witnesses" on the main menu.

The segment ends when Hebrews 12:1 appears on the screen. If the DVD does not return to the main menu by itself, return to the main menu page.

Notes

Therefore, since we are surrounded by such a great cloud of witnesses, let us throw off everything that hinders and the sin that so easily entangles. And let us run with perseverance the race marked out for us.

Hebrews 12:1

DISCUSSION (8 minutes)

You just heard stories of the following people:

- ❖ *Francis of Assisi* and the leper

- ❖ *Madame Guyon* and the smallpox that ruined her face

- ❖ *Frances de Sales* and the speaking statue

- ❖ *Teresa of Avila* talking to God four hours a day

- ❖ *Julian of Norwich* picking up the chestnut

- ❖ *Evelyn Underhill*, first female professor at Oxford University and the "thin place" called Iona in Scotland

- ❖ *Brother Lawrence,* the pot scrubber at the monastery and the gale wind of the Holy Spirit

- ❖ *Augustine* and the "house of the soul" being too small

- ❖ *C. S. Lewis* saying, "I want God, not my idea of God"

Discuss the following questions:

- ❖ In what ways were these individuals "ordinary people" like you and me?

- ❖ Whose life or story do you most relate to? What ideas or impressions did you have as you heard that person's story?

PLAY DVD (7 minutes)

On the main menu select "Alone with the Lord." This segment explores *lectio divina* as a personal practice. The framework is included on page 61 so you do not have to write it down—just concentrate on the DVD and jot down any additional thoughts you might have.

Notes

Then He said, "Go out, and stand on the mountain before the LORD." And behold, the LORD passed by, and a great and strong wind tore into the mountains and broke the rocks in pieces before the LORD, but the LORD was not in the wind; and after the wind an earthquake, but the LORD was not in the earthquake; and after the earthquake a fire, but the LORD was not in the fire; and after the fire a still small voice. So it was, when Elijah heard it, that he wrapped his face in his mantle and went out and stood in the entrance of the cave.

1 Kings 19:11-13a (NKJV)

59

Each of us needs

half an hour of prayer each day,

except when we are busy . . .

then we need an hour.

St. Francis de Sales

INDIVIDUAL PRACTICE (15 minutes)

Use these steps below to help you incorporate *lectio divina* into your personal time alone with the Lord.

PREPARATION

❖ Take your Bible with you and find a quiet corner wherever you are meeting.

❖ Get comfortable but remain alert. Take some deep breaths and relax. Inhale and imagine the Holy Spirit breathing His peace into you; as you exhale, cast your cares on Him.

❖ Open your Bible to Psalm 1:1–3 or to 1 John 1:5–7.

PRACTICE

❖ Read whatever passage you chose out loud, slowly and deliberately, four different times. Allow a minute or two of silence between each reading to let the Word of God permeate your heart. Use the steps below as a guide to your reading.

Read: Simply listen to the Word.

Reflect: What touches my life today?

Respond: What is God inviting me to do?

Rest: Experience God's presence.

❖ To conclude, you might want to express praise or gratitude, or simply enjoy God and rest in His presence.

DISCUSSION (6 minutes)

Briefly recap the individual practice. What did you experience?

CLOSING THOUGHTS
AND PRAYER (5 minutes)

This concludes your four-session experience with *Be Still*. It is our prayer that learning about and practicing contemplative prayer has been a deepening and enriching experience. We hope you will want to incorporate *lectio divina* into your group, and your personal prayer times, on a regular basis.

If you have more than sixty minutes, we encourage you to talk about what you've learned and share how these four sessions have impacted your relationship with God and with each other.

Close the meeting in prayer.

Have you ever thought what a wonderful privilege it is that everyone each day and each hour of the day has the liberty of asking God to meet him in the inner chamber and to hear what He was to say? We should imagine that every Christian would use such a privilege gladly and faithfully.

Andrew Murray

ΠΕΧΤ STEPS

Πow that you understand the basics of contemplative prayer, you can continue with the practice either on your own or with your small group. All you really need is a Bible passage, some quiet time and a quiet place. You might want to choose a Scripture from the message that will be preached the following week at church (most churches note next week's message topic in a bulletin or on a Web site). You also might want to choose Scriptures from a Bible study you are doing that you would like to experience in a deeper way, or choose passages that speak to what you might be experiencing personally.

The process of knowing God is not difficult. You don't have to be a saint or scholar to experience His presence more deeply. All it requires is you, God, a Bible and a commitment. However, slowing down to spend time with the Lord will not just happen. It is a choice, and you have to make a plan. Here are a few suggestions to help you take next steps.

- ❖ Identify the best time of the day for you to pray. Give God your best time of day.

- ❖ Let others know it is your quiet time and why it is important that they respect this time.

- ❖ Declutter your quiet time area.

- ❖ Take a noise inventory. As best as you can, eliminate all unnecessary noise in your quiet time area.

- ❖ Have your Bible, a pen and a notebook on hand.

- ❖ Set a timer so you don't need to watch the clock.

- ❖ Take a few deep breaths before you start. Don't race into the Lord's presence. Ask the Holy Spirit to lead you as you pray.

- ❖ Read a favorite psalm aloud to start your time with God.

- ❖ If you don't know what to pray, pray the prayers of the Bible and make them your own. Pray the Psalms. Like all songs, sometimes it is better to speak them aloud for the words to reach the heart.

❖ Change your posture. If you are dozing off regularly in your prayer times, then stand, stretch and walk around the room before you sit to pray.

❖ Download your to-do list. If things pop into your head while you are trying to be still with God, write them down and set them aside. They will still be there when you finish your quiet time.

❖ Remember to stop and breathe throughout the day. Take five deep breaths at the beginning of each hour. Say to yourself, "I am breathing in the Holy Spirit's peace and breathing out all of the cares of the world."

Lord, teach us to pray.
Luke 11:1

❖ Are you anxious? Write down your worries and surrender them to God in prayer.

❖ Accustom yourself to periods of silence and don't be afraid of pauses in conversation.

ADDITIONAL RESOURCES

Richard J. Foster	*Prayer: Finding the Heart's True Home*
	Devotional Classics: Selected Readings for Individuals and Groups on the Twelve Spiritual Disciplines
Ken Gire	*Intimate Moments with the Savior: Learning to Love*
Madame Guyon	*Experiencing the Depths of Jesus Christ*
Brother Lawrence	*The Practice of the Presence of God*
Max Lucado	*Cure for the Common Life: Living in Your Sweet Spot*
Calvin Miller	*Into the Depths of God: Where Eyes See the Invisible, Ears Hear the Inaudible and Minds Conceive the Inconceivable*

John Ortberg	*The Life You've Always Wanted: Spiritual Disciplines for Ordinary People*
Priscilla Shirer	*He Speaks to Me: Preparing to Hear the Voice of God*
	Discerning the Voice of God: How to Recognize When God Speaks
Mother Teresa	*A Simple Path*
Dallas Willard	*Hearing God: Developing a Conversational Relationship with God*
Dallas Willard with Don Simpson	*Revolution of Character: Discovering Christ's Pattern for Spiritual Transformation*

ABOUT THE AUTHORS

BILL DONAHUE

Bill Donahue is executive director of small group ministries for the Willow Creek Association (WCA) and works with Willow Creek Community Church to train and develop small group leaders. He is the author of several bestselling books, including *Leading Life-Changing Small Groups, In the Company of Jesus* and the *Jesus 101* Bible Study Series. He is also co-author with Russ Robinson of *Building a Church of Small Groups, Walking the Small Group Tightrope* and *The Seven Deadly Sins of Small Group Ministry*. Bill has an undergraduate degree in psychology from Princeton University, a masters degree in biblical studies from Dallas Seminary and a Ph.D. in adult learning from the University of North Texas. Bill makes his home in the Chicago suburbs with his wife Gail, son Ryan and daughter Kinsley.

AMY AND JUDGE REINHOLD

Amy and Judge Reinhold are the founders of A Barking Catfish Productions. Together, they wrote, directed and produced the *Be Still* DVD for Twentieth Century Fox. Judge is an Emmy-nominated actor who has been in more than seventy-five films. Amy has an undergraduate degree in English from Southern Methodist University. Amy and Judge have been happily married for eight years and enjoy living in both California and New Mexico.

BE STILL
DVD and Participant's Guide

Be Still is an extraordinary DVD that demonstrates how contemplative, or "listening" prayer, can be a vital way to experience God's guidance and peace in the midst of frenzied, fast-paced lives. The DVD features interviews with some of today's most highly respected Christian leaders, including Max Lucado, Michelle McKinney Hammond, Henry Cloud, Richard Foster, Dallas Willard and more.

This 90-minute DVD is available alone or as a kit. The kit includes a DVD packaged with one *Be Still* Participant's Guide.

DVD: UPC 024543234616
Kit: UPC 633277299336
Participant's Guide: ISBN 0-744-19248-X

Pick up a copy today at your favorite bookstore!

www.bestillprayer.net

WILLOW

www.willowcreek.com

BE STILL
31 Days to a Deeper Meditative Prayer Life

Amy and Judge Reinhold

Be Still: 31 Days to a Deeper Meditative Prayer Life offers daily devotions to help you slow down and connect with God in a more intimate way. Each day's reading includes:

- A quote from one of the "great cloud of witnesses" (throughout Christian history)
- Questions for personal reflection or group discussion
- A message from a *Be Still* DVD contributor or special guest
- A *Be Still* moment for practical application
- A Scripture passage for meditation
- Helpful hints to create quality time with God

Drawing on content from the *Be Still* DVD, the devotional features wisdom from some of today's most highly respected Christian leaders who have experienced the value of quality time spent alone with God. Blank journal pages are also provided for those who find that writing helps them express their thoughts and connect with God.

Hardcover: 1-4165-4590-5

Pick up a copy today at your favorite bookstore!

www.bestillprayer.net

HOWARD BOOKS
A DIVISION OF SIMON & SCHUSTER

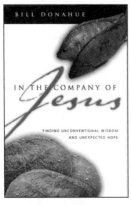

IN THE COMPANY OF JESUS
Finding Unconventional Wisdom and Unexpected Hope

Bill Donahue

In the Company of Jesus brings to life the many facets of who Jesus is and what his work in the world is all about. Written in forty brief segments with opportunities for personal reflection and dialogue with God, the book explores eight ways we encounter Jesus in the gospels and is ideal for daily reading. Whether you are meeting Jesus for the first time or you've known him for many years, you'll find new insights from time spent in the company of Jesus.

In the Company of Jesus is a companion to the *Jesus 101* Bible Study Series.

Hardcover: ISBN 0-8308-3275-0

Pick up a copy today at your favorite bookstore!

JESUS 101 Bible Study Series

Bill Donahue

These eight study guides expand on eight ways we encounter Christ in the gospels, as outlined in the book *In the Company of Jesus*. Each study guide stands alone and provides everything you need to lead six sessions, including leader notes, study questions and group activities.

Softcover:

Jesus: Authentic Leader	ISBN 0-8308-2155-4
Jesus: Compassionate Healer	ISBN 0-8308-2156-2
Jesus: Extreme Forgiver	ISBN 0-8308-2154-6
Jesus: Provocative Teacher	ISBN 0-8308-2151-1
Jesus: Relentless Lover	ISBN 0-8308-2157-0
Jesus: Sacred Friend	ISBN 0-8308-2152-X
Jesus: Supreme Conqueror	ISBN 0-8308-2158-9
Jesus: Truthful Revealer	ISBN 0-8308-2153-8

Pick up a copy today at your favorite bookstore!

IVP Connect
Exploring Faith. Shaping Lives.

WILLOW
www.willowcreek.com

REGROUP
Training Groups to Be Groups

Henry Cloud, Bill Donahue, John Townsend

This groundbreaking, DVD-driven curriculum establishes a new paradigm that simultaneously trains both leaders and group members on what it means to create and sustain a vibrant, life-changing small group. Designed for use in small group meetings—of any size or type—the two training DVDs include expert teaching, modeling dramas, person-on-the-street interviews, personal stories/testimonies, creative multimedia and discussion material. The first DVD leads groups through four foundational 60-minute meetings. The second DVD provides groups with 13 five-minute coaching segments to use at the beginning of subsequent meetings and three 60-minute sessions on three critical issues:

- Resolving conflict
- Uniting around people in pain
- Learning to deal with difficult people

The kit includes two DVDs. Order one Participant's Guide for each person.

DVD Kit: ISBN 0-310-27783-3
Participant's Guide: ISBN 0-310-27785-X

Pick up a copy today at your favorite bookstore!

www.willowcreek.com

LEADING LIFE-CHANGING SMALL GROUPS

Bill Donahue

The most complete and comprehensive tool
for training small group leaders available.
It carries my highest recommendation.

Gareth Icenogle, D.Min., Pasadena International Small Group Consultant;
Adjunct Professor, Fuller Seminary

This best-selling guidebook helps small group leaders cultivate
groups that foster discipleship and spiritual transformation.
Organized in a ready-reference format, you'll find insights on:

- Group formation and values
- Leadership responsibilities
- Meeting preparation and participation
- Discipleship within the group
- Leadership training . . . and much more.

From an individual group to an entire small group ministry,
Leading Life-Changing Small Groups gives you the comprehensive
guidance you need to help people become fully devoted followers
of Christ.

Softcover: ISBN 0-310-24750-0

Pick up a copy today at your favorite bookstore!

www.willowcreek.com

Willow Creek Association

WILLOW
Willow Creek Resources

Vision, Training, Resources for Prevailing Churches

This resource was created to serve you and to help you build a local church that prevails. It is just one of many ministry tools that are part of the Willow Creek Resources® line.

The Willow Creek Association (WCA) was created in 1992 to serve a rapidly growing number of churches from across the denominational spectrum that are committed to helping unchurched people become fully-devoted followers of Christ. Membership in the WCA now numbers over 12,000 Member Churches worldwide from more than ninety denominations.

The Willow Creek Association links like-minded Christian leaders with each other and with strategic vision, training and resources in order to help them build prevailing churches designed to reach their redemptive potential. Here are some of the ways the WCA does that.

The Leadership Summit—A once a year, two-and-a-half-day learning experience to envision and equip Christians with leadership gifts and responsibilities. Presented live on Willow's campus as well as via satellite simulcast to over 135 locations across North America—plus more than eighty international cities feature the Summit by way of videocast every Fall—this event is designed to increase the leadership effectiveness of pastors, ministry staff, volunteer church leaders and Christians in the marketplace.

Ministry-Specific Conferences—Throughout the year the WCA hosts a variety of conferences and training events—both at Willow Creek's main campus and offsite, across North America and around the world. These events are for church leaders and volunteers in areas such as group life, children's ministry, student ministry, preaching and teaching, the arts and stewardship.

Willow Creek Resources®—Provides churches with trusted and field-tested ministry resources on important topics such as leadership, volunteer ministries, spiritual formation, stewardship, evangelism, group life, children's ministry, student ministry, the arts and more.

WCA Member Benefits—Includes substantial discounts to WCA training events, a 20 percent discount on all Willow Creek Resources®, *Defining Moments* monthly audio journal for leaders, quarterly *Willow* magazine, access to a Members-Only section on WCA's web site, monthly communications and more. Member Churches also receive special discounts and premier services through the WCA's growing number of ministry partners—Select Service Providers—and save an average of $500 annually depending on the level of engagement.

For specific information about WCA conferences, resources, membership, and other ministry services, contact:

Willow Creek Association
P.O. Box 3188, Barrington, IL 60011-3188
Phone: 847-570-9812 • Fax: 847-765-5046
www.willowcreek.com

We want to hear from you.

Please send your comments about this resource

to us in care of info@bestillprayer.net. Thank you.

WILLOW
www.willowcreek.com

BE STILL
www.bestillprayer.net